www.mrmen.com

Mr. Men and Little Miss™ Text and illustrations
© 2010 THOIP (a Chorion company).
Printed and published under licence from
Price Stern Sloan, Inc., Los Angeles.

Original creation by Roger Hargreaves
Illustrated by Adam Hargreaves
First published in Great Britain 1998
This edition published in Great Britain in 2010 by Dean,
an imprint of Egmont UK Limited
239 Kensington High Street, London W8 6SA

Printed in Italy
ISBN 978 0 6035 6569 4

1 3 5 7 9 10 8 6 4 2

LITTLE MISS SPLENDID

AND THE HOUSE WITH A VIEW

Roger Hargreaves

DEAN

Little Miss Splendid looked out of her very splendid window, set in her most splendid house, at her very splendid garden, and smiled.

And then she frowned.

Little Miss Splendid looked out of her window every morning and every morning she smiled and then she frowned.

And what made her frown?

I'll tell you.

At the bottom of her garden, on the other side of a small stream, lived Mr Mean.

Unlike Miss Splendid's very large and most splendid house, Mr Mean's house is very small and very run down.

A not at all splendid house.

In fact, the most un-splendid house one could ever imagine.

Mr Mean was the sort of person who did not like spending money, especially on his house.

Little Miss Splendid was the complete opposite.

And she did not like having Mr Mean as a neighbour.

His house quite ruined her splendid view.

It was on this particular morning as she stood looking out of her window that Miss Splendid had an idea.

She rang her builder, Mr Trowel.

"Hello," she said, "This is Miss Splendid. I would like you to build a wall for me. Come at once."

Mr Trowel came over within an hour and within a day he had built a wall at the bottom of Little Miss Splendid's garden.

A high wall.

A wall that hid Mr Mean's house.

Now, Mr Mean also liked to look out of his window each morning.

He had a splendid view of Miss Splendid's extraordinarily splendid house.

And what made the view all
the more splendid
for Mr Mean was
the fact that
it hadn't cost
him a penny.

...g when Little Miss
...out of the window
...ve her eyes.

Mr
lo
a

The next mornin
Splendid looked
she couldn't belie

There was a huge hole in her beautiful wall and through the hole she could see Mr Mean's ramshackle house.

Miss Splendid was furious.

She rang Mr Trowel immediately and by lunch-time Mr Trowel had rebuilt the wall.

But the next morning there was another hole in her wall.

And so it went on all week.

Overnight Mr Mean would knock a hole in the wall and the next day Mr Trowel would come and repair it.

And then one morning the whole wall
had disappeared.

But not just the wall.

There was no sign of Mr Mean's house
either!

"That's strange," said Miss Splendid to herself. She put on her best hat and went to investigate.

When she got down to where Mr Mean's house had been she heard the sound of building coming from the other side of the hill. She climbed to the top of the hill.

And for the second time she couldn't believe her eyes.

There was Mr Busy putting the finishing touches to a house that looked liked hers, but was even more splendid!

"Looks good, doesn't it?" said a voice behind her.

It was Mr Mean.

"What ... what ... how?" spluttered Miss Splendid.

"It was all those bricks that gave me the idea," said Mr Mean and grinned. "All those free bricks!"

Little Miss Splendid didn't know what to say.

So she didn't say anything.

And she went home.

To her splendid house.

A splendid house, but no longer the most splendid house!